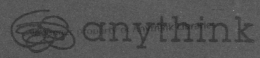

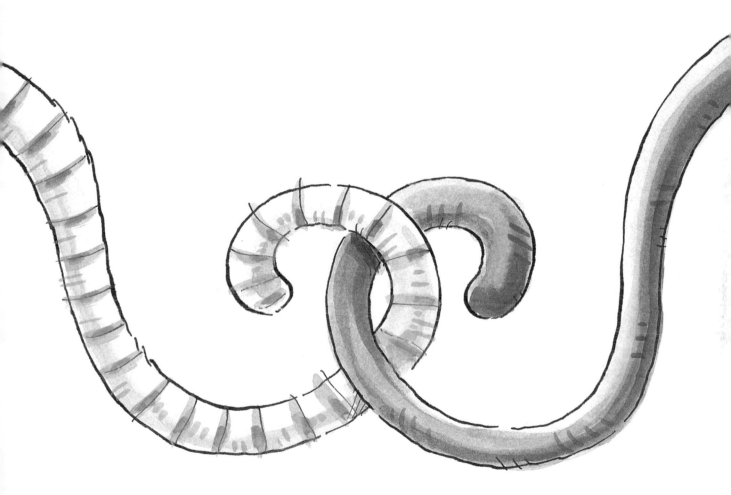

BY SUSAN VERDE · ART BY PETER H. REYNOLDS

Abrams Books for Young Readers

New York

You and Me

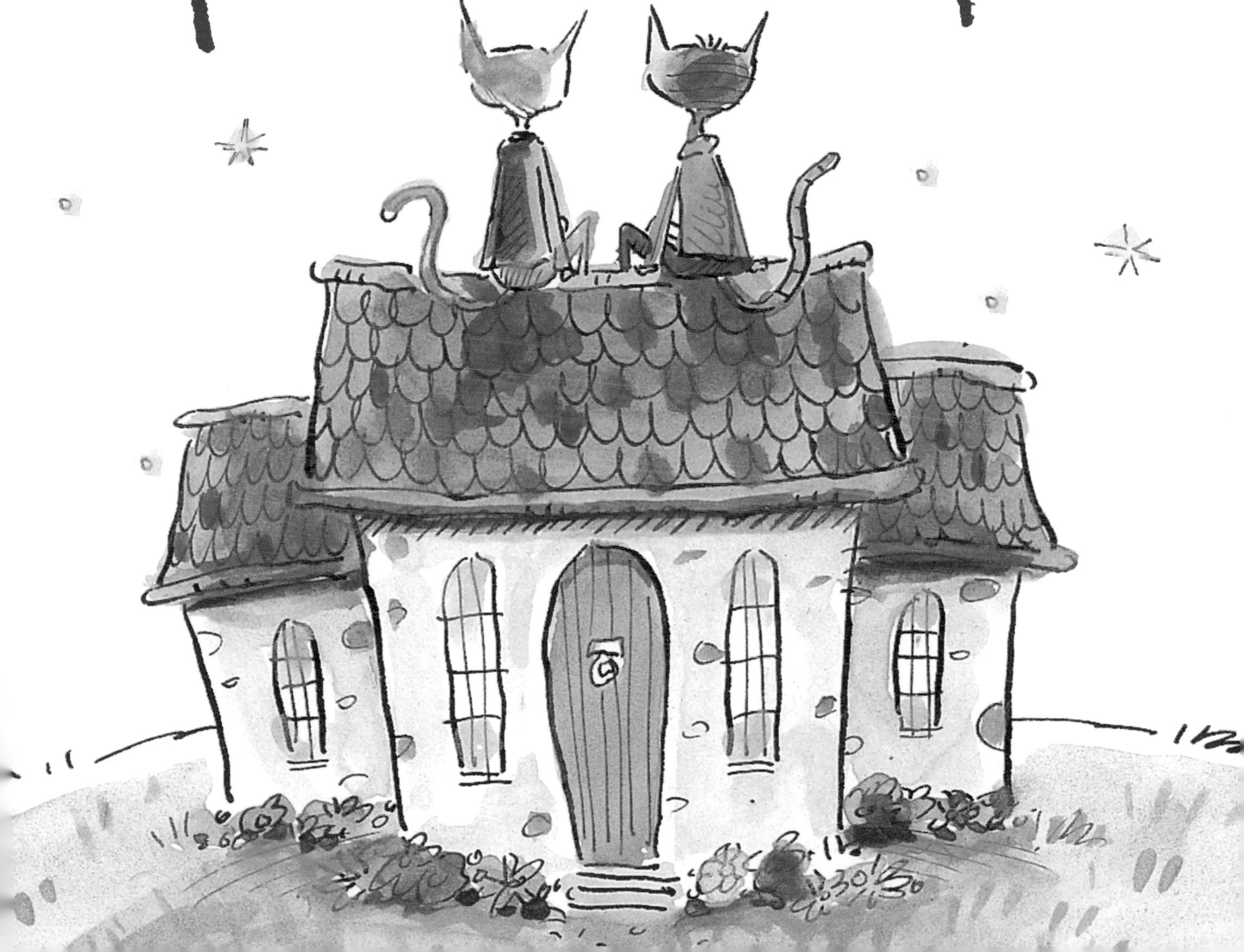

The illustrations in this book were created
using ink, gouache, watercolor, and tea.

Library of Congress Cataloging-in-Publication

Verde, Susan.
You and me / by Susan Verde ;
illustrated by Peter H. Reynolds.
pages cm
Summary: Relates, in rhyming verse, how
fate brought two best friends together.
ISBN 978-1-4197-1197-8
[1. Stories in rhyme. 2. Best friends—Fiction. 3. Friendship—
Fiction. 4. Fate and fatalism—Fiction. 5. Cats—Fiction.]
I. Reynolds, Peter, 1961– illustrator. II. Title.
PZ8.3.V712638Yo 2014
[E]—dc23
2014000491

Text copyright © 2015 Susan Verde
Illustrations copyright © 2015 Peter H. Reynolds
Book design by Chad W. Beckerman

Printed and bound in China
10 9 8 7 6 5 4 3 2 1

Abrams Books for Young Readers are available at special discounts when purchased in quantity for premiums
and promotions as well as fundraising or educational
use. Special editions can also be created to specification.
For details, contact specialsales@abramsbooks.com or the
address below.

ABRAMS
THE ART OF BOOKS SINCE 1949

115 West 18th Street
New York, NY 10011
www.abramsbooks.com

For all the friends on the path of life who fill our hearts
and change our lives, with a special nod
to P.H.R., H.N.S., and M.S.S., without whose friendship
I would "ache in my heart." —S.V.

To Diana —P.H.R.

Sometimes I think
of how things came to be.

How we met. How we became best friends.
You and me.

If that day had chosen
a different way to unfold,

ours is a story that
might not have been told.

What if I had slept in,
covers pulled up to my chin?

If I had sung opera
in the shower

or filled a vase with
fresh-cut flowers...

Or if the clock had been slow and I was late,

lingering over my breakfast plate.

What if the weather had been stormy gray?

I might not have left the house that day.

What if my bicycle had a flat?

Or if I hadn't gone back to fetch my hat.

If a cloud in the sky...

...or a rock in my shoe
had caused me to pause
for a moment or two.

Any of these could have kept us apart!

The very idea makes me ache in my heart.

Whatever it was
that brought us
together...

That pull, that tug, that mysterious tether.

Serendipity,
perfect timing,
all the stars
aligning.

It paved the way for an ideal situation.

A delightful blend, a sublime combination.

I'm so grateful for each step and each choice
that led me to you, your spirit, your voice.

Feeling as one when we're actually two.

Forever
friends...

...me and you.